TIDY
TITCH

TIDY
TITCH

by PAT HUTCHINS

RED FOX

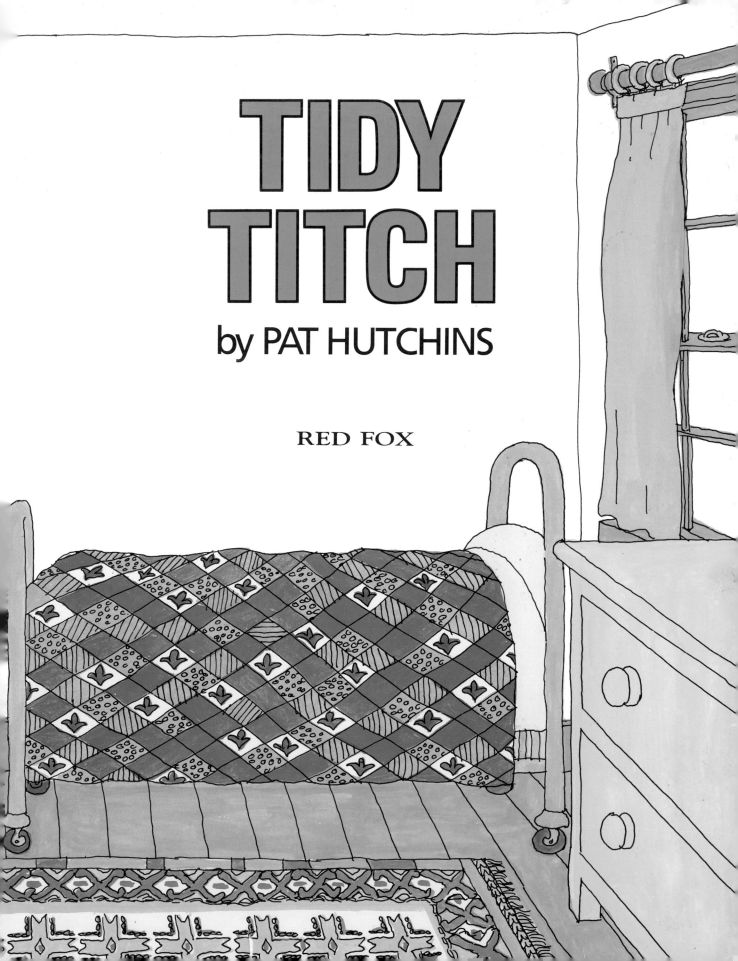

Also by Pat Hutchins

Titch
You'll Soon Grow into Them, Titch
Titch and Daisy
We're Going on a Picnic!
Rosie's Walk
The Shrinking Mouse
Don't Forget the Bacon
Ten Red Apples

TIDY TITCH
A Red Fox Book: 0 09 920741 9

First published in Great Britain by Julia MacRae Books,
an imprint of Random House Children's Books

Julia MacRae edition published 1991
Red Fox edition 1993; this edition 2002

7 9 10 8 6

Red Fox Books are published by Random House Children's Books,
61-63 Uxbridge Road, London W5 5SA,
a division of The Random House Group Ltd,
in Australia by Random House Australia (Pty) Ltd,
20 Alfred Street, Milsons Point, Sydney, NSW 2061, Australia,
in New Zealand by Random House New Zealand Ltd,
18 Poland Road, Glenfield, Auckland 10, New Zealand,
and in South Africa by Random House (Pty) Ltd,
Endulini, 5A Jubilee Road, Parktown 2193, South Africa

THE RANDOM HOUSE GROUP Limited Reg. No. 954009
www.kidsatrandomhouse.co.uk

A CIP catalogue record for this book is available from the British Library.

Printed in Singapore

FOR DAISY GOUNDRY

TIDY
TITCH

"How tidy Titch's room is,"
said Mother to Peter and Mary.
"And how messy your rooms are.
I think you should tidy them up."

"I'll help," said Titch
    as Mother went downstairs.

"I think I'll throw this
   dolls' house out," said Mary,
"and these toys.
   I'm too old for them!"
"I'm not," said Titch.
"I'll have them!"

And Titch carried the dolls' house
and the toys to his room.

"I think I'll throw that old
space suit out," said Peter,
"and that cowboy outfit.
They're much too small for me!"
"They're not too small for me!"
said Titch. "I'll have them!"

And Titch carried the space suit
and the cowboy outfit to his room.

"My room is still untidy," said Mary.
"I think I'll get rid of this broken pram
and these old games.
I've played them hundreds of times!"

"I haven't," said Titch.
"I'll have them!"

And Titch took the pram
and old games to his room.

"My room is still a mess," said Peter.
"I think I'll get rid of
   these old toys. I don't play
   with them any more!"
"I will!" said Titch.
"I'll have them!"

And Titch carried the old toys to his room.

"How neat your rooms are!" said Mother
when she came back upstairs.

"I thought Titch was going to help you."

"He did," said Peter and Mary.